Simple Machines to the Rescue

Inclined Planes to the Rescue

by Sharon Thales

Consultant:
Louis A. Bloomfield, PhD
Professor of Physics
University of Virginia
Charlottesville, Virginia

Capstone
press®
Mankato, Minnesota

First Facts is published by Capstone Press,
1710 Roe Crest Drive, North Mankato, Minnesota 56003.
www.capstonepub.com

Library of Congress Cataloging-in-Publication Data
Thales, Sharon.
    Inclined planes to the rescue / Sharon Thales.
    p. cm.—(First facts. Simple machines to the rescue)
    Summary: "Describes inclined planes, including what they are, how they work, and common
uses of these simple machines today"—Provided by publisher.
    Includes bibliographical references and index.
    ISBN-13: 978-0-7368-6752-8 (hardcover)
    ISBN-10: 0-7368-6752-X (hardcover)
    1. Inclined planes—Juvenile literature. I. Title. II. Series.
TJ147.T42 2007
621.8—dc22   2006021500

Editorial Credits
Becky Viaene, editor; Thomas Emery, designer; Kyle Grenz, illustrator; Jo Miller,
    photo researcher/photo editor

Photo Credits
AP/Wide World Photos/Paul Sancya, 20
Art Directors/Helene Rogers, 6
Aurora/Outdoor Collection/PatitucciPhoto, 10–11
Capstone Press/TJ Thoraldson Digital Photography, cover, 18, 21 (all)
Corbis/David Stoecklein, 5
The Image Works/New Haven Register/Arnold Gold, 12–13
Mary Evans Picture Library/Douglas McCarthy, 9
PhotoEdit Inc./Jeff Greenberg, 19
UNICORN Stock Photos/Gary L. Johnson, 14

Printed in the United States of America in North Mankato, Minnesota.
112012   007025R

Table of Contents

A Helpful Inclined Plane

Your school ski trip is almost over. How can you get to the bottom of the hill before the bus leaves?

Inclined plane to the rescue!

The hill is an **inclined plane**. It can help you get to the bus in a hurry.

Work It

An inclined plane is a **simple machine**. Simple machines have one or no moving parts. Machines are used to make **work** easier.

Work is using a **force** to move an object. Inclined planes make moving heavy items from one level to another easier. They have been used for thousands of years.

Inclined Plane Fact

Not sure what an inclined plane looks like? An inclined plane is a flat surface. It slants up or down from one end to the other.

An Inclined Plane in Time

People in ancient Egypt built giant pyramids. They used millions of stone blocks. Most blocks were heavier than a car. How did Egyptians move and stack such heavy stones? Many people think the Egyptians pushed and pulled the blocks along inclined planes.

Inclined Plane Fact

The longer an inclined plane is, the easier it is to move an object along it. The object has farther to go, but it takes less force to move it.

9

Early humans needed an easy way to move up and down mountains. They saw animals make zigzag paths up mountains. These inclined planes were long, but they made it easier to cross the mountains. Today, people still use zigzag paths to travel on mountains.

What Would We Do Without Inclined Planes?

Every day, millions of people in wheelchairs use inclined planes. Wheelchairs can't go up or down steps, but they can be rolled on ramps. Ramps are inclined planes that help people move safely to different levels.

Want to show your friends your new skateboard moves?

Inclined plane to the rescue!

Skateboard ramps are inclined planes that help you move up and down. Push off the top of the skateboard ramp. You'll quickly move to the bottom of this inclined plane.

Working Together

An escalator is a **complex machine**. It has several simple machines that create a moving inclined plane. An escalator has pulleys at the top and bottom. The pulleys and the motor move the handrail and the chain connecting the steps. Each step has wheels on an axle. The wheels and axles move along this inclined plane.

Inclined Plane Buddies

Six kinds of simple machines combine to make almost every machine there is.

- **Inclined plane**–a slanting surface that is used to move objects to different levels

- **Lever**–a bar that turns on a resting point and is used to lift items

- **Pulley**–a grooved wheel turned by a rope, belt, or chain that often moves heavy objects

- **Screw**–an inclined plane wrapped around a post that usually holds objects together

- **Wedge**–an inclined plane that moves to split things apart or push them together

- **Wheel and axle**–a wheel that turns around a bar to move objects

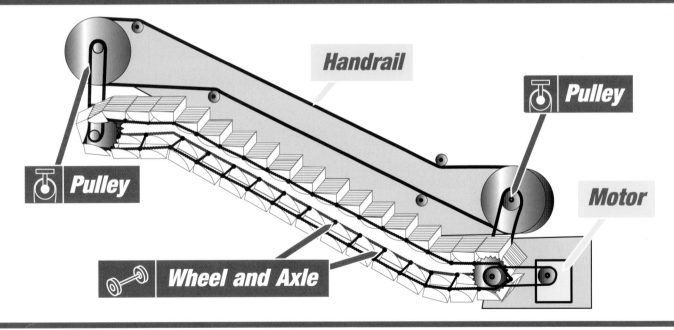

Handrail

Pulley

Pulley

Motor

Wheel and Axle

Inclined Planes Everywhere

Inclined planes can be lots of fun.
Playground slides are inclined planes.
They help you move down quickly.

Ready for a roller coaster ride? Carts filled with screaming people zoom up and down these inclined planes.

Inclined planes can be huge. Parking ramps are inclined planes with many levels. One of the world's largest parking ramps is at the Detroit airport in Michigan. This tall ramp has 10 levels and 11,500 parking spots.

Hands On: Working with an Inclined Plane

What You Need
pile of books, 1 long book, scissors, elastic band, 4 spoons, ruler

What You Do
1. Place the pile of books on the floor. Take the long book and put one end on the pile of books and the other end on the floor. This book is your inclined plane.
2. Use the scissors to cut the elastic band once.
3. Stack the spoons. Tie and knot one end of the elastic around the stack.
4. Pinch the other end of the elastic between your finger and thumb. Lift your hand until the spoons are hanging just above the middle of the inclined plane.
5. Use the ruler to measure the elastic from the spoons to your finger.
6. Next, pull the elastic to drag the spoons up the inclined plane. When the spoons are halfway up, measure again from elastic to finger. Is the elastic longer or shorter than when you lifted the spoons straight up?

The length of the stretched elastic increases when more force is needed. So which took less force?

21

Glossary

complex machine (KOM-pleks muh-SHEEN)—a machine made of two or more simple machines

force (FORSS)—a push or a pull

inclined plane (in-KLINDE PLANE)—a slanting surface that is used to move objects to different levels

simple machine (SIM-puhl muh-SHEEN)—a tool with one or no moving parts that moves an object when you push or pull; inclined planes are simple machines.

work (WURK)—when a force moves an object

Read More

Tieck, Sarah. *Inclined Planes.* Simple Machines. Edina, Minn.: Abdo, 2006.

Tiner, John Hudson. *Inclined Planes.* Simple Machines. North Mankato, Minn.: Smart Apple Media, 2003.

Walker, Sally M. and Roseann Feldmann. *Inclined Planes and Wedges.* Early Bird Physics. Minneapolis: Lerner, 2002.

Internet Sites

FactHound offers a safe, fun way to find Internet sites related to this book. All of the sites on FactHound have been researched by our staff.

Here's how:

1. Visit *www.facthound.com*

2. Choose your grade level.

3. Type in this book ID **073686752X** for age-appropriate sites. You may also browse subjects by clicking on letters, or by clicking on pictures and words.

4. Click on the **Fetch It** button.

FactHound will fetch the best sites for you!

Index